WITCH POEMS

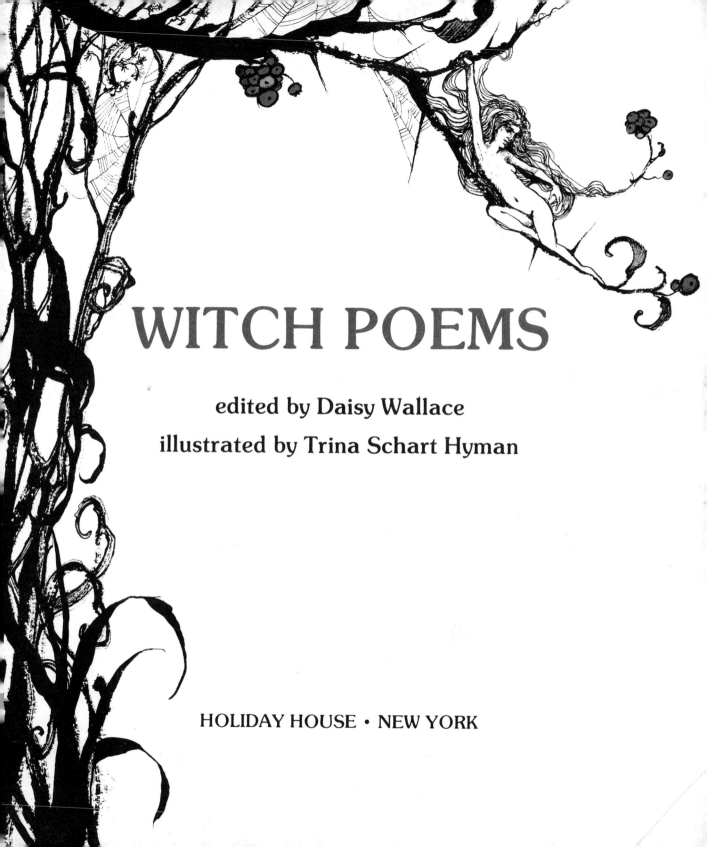

WITCH POEMS

edited by Daisy Wallace

illustrated by Trina Schart Hyman

HOLIDAY HOUSE • NEW YORK

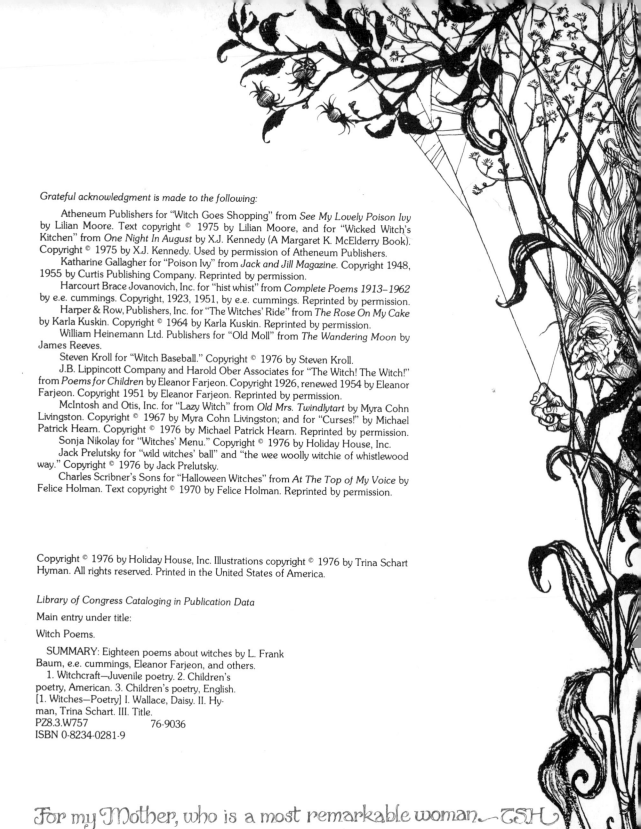

Grateful acknowledgment is made to the following:

Atheneum Publishers for "Witch Goes Shopping" from *See My Lovely Poison Ivy* by Lilian Moore. Text copyright © 1975 by Lilian Moore, and for "Wicked Witch's Kitchen" from *One Night In August* by X.J. Kennedy (A Margaret K. McElderry Book). Copyright © 1975 by X.J. Kennedy. Used by permission of Atheneum Publishers.

Katharine Gallagher for "Poison Ivy" from *Jack and Jill Magazine*. Copyright 1948, 1955 by Curtis Publishing Company. Reprinted by permission.

Harcourt Brace Jovanovich, Inc. for "hist whist" from *Complete Poems 1913–1962* by e.e. cummings. Copyright, 1923, 1951, by e.e. cummings. Reprinted by permission.

Harper & Row, Publishers, Inc. for "The Witches' Ride" from *The Rose On My Cake* by Karla Kuskin. Copyright © 1964 by Karla Kuskin. Reprinted by permission.

William Heinemann Ltd. Publishers for "Old Moll" from *The Wandering Moon* by James Reeves.

Steven Kroll for "Witch Baseball." Copyright © 1976 by Steven Kroll.

J.B. Lippincott Company and Harold Ober Associates for "The Witch! The Witch!" from *Poems for Children* by Eleanor Farjeon. Copyright 1926, renewed 1954 by Eleanor Farjeon. Copyright 1951 by Eleanor Farjeon. Reprinted by permission.

McIntosh and Otis, Inc. for "Lazy Witch" from *Old Mrs. Twindlytart* by Myra Cohn Livingston. Copyright © 1967 by Myra Cohn Livingston; and for "Curses!" by Michael Patrick Hearn. Copyright © 1976 by Michael Patrick Hearn. Reprinted by permission.

Sonja Nikolay for "Witches' Menu." Copyright © 1976 by Holiday House, Inc.

Jack Prelutsky for "wild witches' ball" and "the wee woolly witchie of whistlewood way." Copyright © 1976 by Jack Prelutsky.

Charles Scribner's Sons for "Halloween Witches" from *At The Top of My Voice* by Felice Holman. Text copyright © 1970 by Felice Holman. Reprinted by permission.

Library of Congress Cataloging in Publication Data

Main entry under title:

Witch Poems.

SUMMARY: Eighteen poems about witches by L. Frank Baum, e.e. cummings, Eleanor Farjeon, and others.
1. Witchcraft—Juvenile poetry. 2. Children's poetry, American. 3. Children's poetry, English. [1. Witches—Poetry] I. Wallace, Daisy. II. Hyman, Trina Schart. III. Title.
PZ8.3.W757   76-9036
ISBN 0-8234-0281-9

For my Mother, who is a most remarkable woman.—TSH

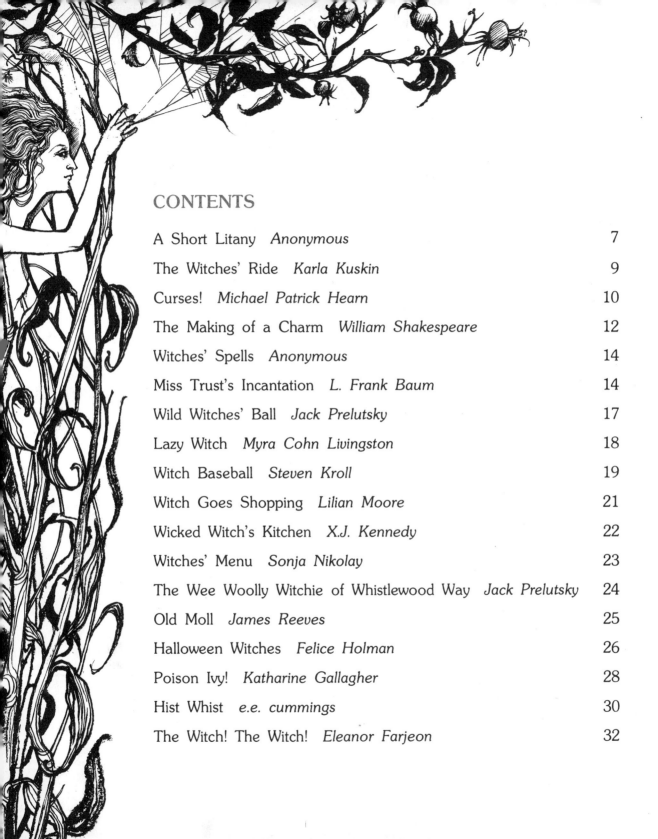

CONTENTS

A SHORT LITANY

From witches and wizards and longtail'd buzzards
And creeping things that run in hedge bottoms
Good Lord deliver us.

ANONYMOUS

7

THE WITCHES' RIDE

Over the hills
Where the edge of light
Deepens and darkens
To ebony night,
Narrow hats high
Above yellow bead eyes,
The tatter-haired witches
Ride through the skies.
Over the seas
Where the flat fishes sleep
Wrapped in the slap of the slippery deep,
Over the peaks
Where the black trees are bare,
Where boney birds quiver
They glide through the air.
Silently humming
A horrible tune,
They sweep through the stillness
To sit on the moon.

KARLA KUSKIN

9

CURSES!

First Witch:

Ragwort, tansy, parsley, pea!
    You'd better stay away from me!
Purple pumpkins, crabgrass green!
    You're the ugliest thing I've ever seen!
Bumble,
Grumble,
Mumblety peg!
Let a worm crawl up your leg!
Brooklyn needle,
Jersey pin!
Let a snail sit on your chin!
    Nyeh!

10

CURSES!

Second Witch:
Oh, pickle water!
Penguin toes!
Let your nose grow like a gardenia grows!
Six times six,
And two times two!
    Let your hair turn blue!
    Let your hair turn blue!
    Let it stick like glue!
And if you think that's bad,
    If you think that's bad,
    If you think *that's* bad,
Here's something worse:
You'll never get free of *my* witch's curse!
    So there!

MICHAEL PATRICK HEARN

THE MAKING OF A CHARM

Round about the cauldron go:
In the poisoned entrails throw.
Toad, that under cold stone
Days and nights has thirty-one
Sweltered venom sleeping got
Boil thou first i' th' charméd pot!

Double, double toil and trouble;
Fire burn and cauldron bubble.
Fillet of a fenny snake,
In the cauldron boil and bake:
Eye of newt and toe of frog,
Wool of bat and tongue of dog,
Adder's fork and blind-worm's sting,
Lizard's leg and howlet's wing,
For a charm of powerful trouble,
Like a hell-broth boil and bubble.

Double, double toil and trouble;
Fire burn and cauldron bubble.
Cool it with a baboon's blood,
Then the charm is firm and good.

WILLIAM SHAKESPEARE
from *Macbeth*. Act IV. Scene 1

12

WITCHES' SPELLS

Miss Trust's Incantation

Erig-a-ma-role, erig-a-ma-ree;
Jig-ger-nut, jog-ger-nit, que-jig-ger-ee.
Sim-mer-kin, sam-mer-kin, sem-mer-ga-roo;
Zil-li-pop, zel-li-pop, lol-li-pop-loo!

L. FRANK BAUM
from *Queen Zixi of Ix*

14

Mounting their broomsticks:

Horse and hattock,
Horse and go,
Horse and pelatis, Ho, ho!

To raise a wind:

I knok this rag upone this stane
To raise the wind in the divellis name;
It shall not lye till I please againe.

To make their enchanted horses
fly through the sky:

Tout, tout,
Throughout and about.

15

WILD WITCHES' BALL

late last night at wildwitchhall
we witches held our wild witch ball.
in every size and shape and weight
we witches came to celebrate.

ten tall crones with moans and groans
battled in barrels with bats and bones.
nine queer dears with pointed ears
dangled and swang from the chandeliers.

witches eight with mangy tresses
danced with seven sorceresses.
witches six in shaggy rags
played toss and tag with five old hags.

four fat bags took healthy bites
from parts of three unsightly frights.
two fierce furies dug a ditch
and tumbled in one lumpy witch.

there were witches squeezed in every nook
whichever where you cared to look.
how many witches can you see
at our annual wildwitch witches' spree?

JACK PRELUTSKY

17

LAZY WITCH

Lazy witch
What's wrong with you?
> Get up and stir your magic brew.
> Here's candlelight to chase the gloom.
> Jump up and mount your flying broom
> And muster up your charms and spells
> And wicked grins and piercing yells.
> It's Halloween! There's work to do!

Lazy witch,
What's wrong with you?

MYRA COHN LIVINGSTON

18

WITCH BASEBALL

The game's the same
But ghouls make the rules
And witches dig ditches
To rescue wild pitches.

On brooms they zoom
To bases with faces
And pitches with twitches
Put batters in stitches.

After each inning
The witches go swimming.

STEVEN KROLL

19

GAME
TONIGHT!
→
SCREAMING MIMIS
VS.
THE BLACK SOX

WITCH GOES SHOPPING

Witch rides off
Upon her broom
Finds a space
To park it.
Takes a shiny shopping cart
Into the supermarket.
Smacks her lips and reads
The list of things she needs:

    "Six bats' wings
    Worms in brine
    Ears of toads
    Eight or nine.
    Slugs and bugs
    Snake skins dried
    Buzzard innards
    Pickled, fried."

Witch takes herself
From shelf to shelf
Cackling all the while.
Up and down and up and down and
In and out each aisle.
Out come cans and cartons
Tumbling to the floor.
"This," says Witch, now all a-twitch
"Is a crazy store.
I CAN'T FIND A SINGLE THING
I AM LOOKING FOR!"

LILIAN MOORE

21

WICKED WITCH'S KITCHEN

You're in the mood for freaky food?
You feel your taste buds itchin'
For nice fresh poison ivy greens?
Try Wicked Witch's kitchen!

She has corn on the cobweb, cauldron-hot,
She makes the meanest cider,
But her broomstick cakes and milkweed shakes
Aren't fit to feed a spider.

She likes to brew hot toadstool stew—
"Come eat, my sweet!" she'll cackle—
But if you do, you'll turn into
A jack-o-lantern's jackal.

X.J. KENNEDY

22

WITCHES' MENU

Live lizard, dead lizard
Marinated, fried.
Poached lizard, pickled lizard
Salty lizard hide.

Hot lizard, cold lizard
Lizard over ice.
Baked lizard, boiled lizard
Lizard served with spice.

Sweet lizard, sour lizard
Smoked lizard heart.
Leg of lizard, loin of lizard
Lizard a la carte.

SONJA NIKOLAY

23

THE WEE WOOLLY WITCHIE
OF WHISTLEWOOD WAY

i'm the wee woolly witchie of whistlewood way
only ten tiny inches in height
i dare to go out only during the day
for i'm frightfully frightened of night
and instead of dull black
wear a woolly white sack
i'm the wee woolly witchie of whistlewood way

i'm the wee woolly witchie of whistlewood way
but my witchery doesn't work well
though i fix up a mix of elixir each day
i have seldom cast one single spell
i find little success
all my magic's a mess
i'm the wee woolly witchie of whistlewood way

i'm the wee woolly witchie of whistlewood way
i'd be better off staying in bed
my attempts to turn tin into gold go astray
i turn tin into tinsel instead
though i'll never get rich
i'm one wonderful witch
i'm the wee woolly witchie of whistlewood way

JACK PRELUTSKY

24

OLD MOLL

The moon is up,
　　The night owls scritch.
Who's that croaking?
　　The frog in the ditch.
Who's that howling?
　　The old hound bitch.
My neck tingles,
　　My elbows itch,
My hair rises,
　　My eyelids twitch.
What's in that pot
　　So rare and rich?
Who's that crouching
　　In a cloak like pitch?
Hush! that's Old Moll—
　　They say she's a
Most ree-markable old party.

JAMES REEVES

25

HALLOWEEN WITCHES

Magical prognosticator,
Chanting, canting, calculator,
Exorcist and necromancer,
Venificial, sabbat dancer,
Striga, arted and capricious,
Conjurer and *maleficius*.
      Tonight, how many witches fly?
      How many brooms will sweep the sky?

FELICE HOLMAN

26

POISON IVY!

A wicked witch
Is Mizzable Scratch,
And it's TROUBLE she grows
In her garden patch.
And her garden patch
Lies all around,
For she grows Poison Ivy!

By ditch and fence
She leaves her trail,
As she sows her seed
Over hill and dale,
And her crop of mischief
Can never fail,
For she grows Poison Ivy!

28

So listen, my children,
Take heed, be good,
And if ever you roam
Through a tangled wood,
Or follow a road,
Some lovely day,
Over the hills and far away,
Please keep out
Of the garden patch
Sown and grown by Mizzable Scratch,
Or it's TROUBLE you will surely catch,
For she grows Poison Ivy!

KATHERINE GALLAGHER

HIST WHIST

hist   whist
little ghostthings
tip-toe
twinkle-toe

little twitchy
witches and tingling
goblins
hob-a-nob   hob-a-nob

little hoppy happy
toad in tweeds
tweeds
little itchy mousies

with scuttling
eyes   rustle and run   and
hidehidehide
whisk

whisk   look out for the old woman
with the wart on her nose
what she'll do to yer
nobody knows

30

for she knows the devil   ooch
the devil   ouch
the devil
ach   the great

green
dancing
devil
devil

devil
devil

          wheeEEE

                    E.E. CUMMINGS

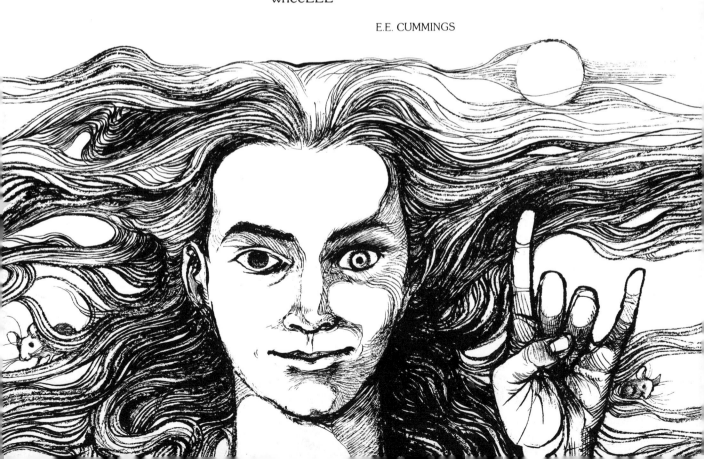

THE WITCH! THE WITCH!

The Witch! The Witch! don't let her get you!
Or your Aunt wouldn't know you the next time she met you!

ELEANOR FARJEON